LEGENDS OF

CHIMA ™

THE WARRIOR WITHIN

Scholastic Inc.

"The Traitor and the Trap," "The Best of Enemies," and "The Vault"
written by Greg Farshtey. Adapted by Anna Holmes.

Illustrated by Ameet Studio

ISBN 978-0-545-62787-0

12 11 10 9 8 7 6 5 4 3 2   14 15 16 17 18 19/0
Printed in the U.S.A.   40

First Scholastic printing, January 2014

TABLE OF CONTENTS

Not long ago, the tribes of Chima™ lived in peace and harmony. We shared CHI, the incredible life-force that built our civilization, equally amongst ourselves. But times have changed. Today we must fight to protect the CHI.

Believe it or not, the conflict began with an innocent prank. My son, Laval, and his best friend Cragger, the Crocodile Prince, snuck into the Lion Temple. At first, they only wanted to see the Sacred Pool of CHI. But then, Cragger broke the rules. He stole a CHI Orb, and his prank led to a great battle between the Lions and the Crocodiles. Cragger's father, King Crominus, was accidentally lost in the fight. Now our tribes are enemies. The Crocodiles have vowed to take control of all the CHI, and we Lions are sworn to protect it.

With his father gone, Cragger has become the fearsome leader of his tribe. He has allied with the vicious Wolves and the sneaky Ravens to launch massive assaults on the Lion Temple.

I, LaGravis, the king of the Lions, have called upon the Eagles and the Gorillas to help in our fight. As the guardians of the CHI, we must protect it. For the sake of Chima!

Any tribe member who has reached the Age of Becoming may use CHI. But younger members are prohibited from using it. The CHI is too powerful and can overwhelm them. This is why it was so dangerous when Cragger stole a CHI Orb as a young Croc.

Inhabitants of Chima wear harnesses designed to hold CHI Orbs. When an animal "plugs" an orb of CHI into their harness, they get an instant surge of energy. Their instincts, strength, and speed are all increased.

Immediately after a tribe member plugs CHI, a glow surrounds them in the image of their inner warrior. This is called the "CHI Up" moment. It only lasts for a brief second, but the power of CHI remains for several hours.

After using CHI, a warrior may feel drained. It can be dangerous for a warrior to use CHI continuously during battle, because it will leave them exhausted and vulnerable. Everything in nature has a balance, including the use of CHI.

LaGravis says:

Tribe members' CHI-up moments will glow blue if they have honorable intentions. But they will glow red if there is anger in their hearts.

BATTLE MACHINES

When the ancient inhabitants of Chima first drank CHI, they evolved from four-legged animals into two legged creatures. They became more intelligent, and learned to build incredible machines to improve their lives.

The first vehicles in Chima were Speedorz™. These one-wheeled racers were made out of a special stone powered by CHI. Today, a Speedor is a tribe member's most prized possession.

The tribes also developed machines suited to their specific needs and talents. The Lions created all-terrain vehicles to rumble over jungle ground. The Crocs built ships to navigate the swamp. The Gorillas created "mechs"—machines modeled after their own bodies—to climb and swing from trees. And the Ravens and Eagles invented incredible flying machines.

All of these amazing constructions use CHI for energy. Each tribe originally designed them for transportation, labor, and fun. But today, these vehicles are armored and equipped with cannons for use on the battlefield.

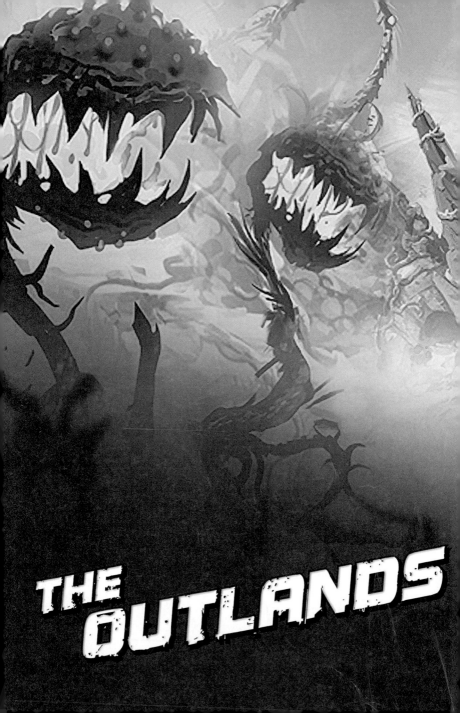

THE OUTLANDS

The Outlands are a dreaded, forbidden zone on the edge of Chima filled with immeasurable dangers. When viewed from a distance, a thick fog shrouds the Outlands in mystery. Strange sounds echo through their depths. Fleeting outlines of unknown creatures scurry by in the mist. Even the bravest warriors fear venturing into this uncharted wasteland.

We do know that small amounts of CHI flow into the Outlands through underground springs. It supplies the plants there with life-forming energy but also twists them into unnatural creatures called Predator Plants. By absorbing the CHI, the Predator Plants gained hunting instincts and strength. Their limbs and roots can attack without warning, posing a constant threat.

But the Predator Plants are only one of the many dangers in the Outlands. No one knows exactly what unimaginable evils lurk farther out in the mist. If anyone has ever ventured out far enough to discover it, they didn't return to tell the tale.

Though many of our ancestors drank the CHI-energized waters, there were some that chose not to drink it. Instead of evolving into more complex creatures, they remained simple and pure. They are known as the Legend Beasts.

According to the Great Story, these animals feared that drinking the CHI and evolving would create more problems than good. Instead of joining our ancestors as they built temples and tribes, the Legend Beasts headed off into the Outlands, never to be seen again.

For centuries, the tale of the Legend Beasts became more and more a myth. Many of the inhabitants of Chima doubted the Legend Beasts ever even existed. But that all changed when the Great Conflict started. During a particularly grueling battle, just as the Crocodiles were about to defeat us, a Lion Legend Beast came to our rescue. Its mere presence was enough to bring the fighting to an end, at least for the time being.

LaGravis says:

My son, Laval, was the one who found the Lion Legend Beast and came to our rescue. That day, he proved he was a true warrior.

THE TRAITOR AND THE TRAP

Laval sprinted toward the Croc Swamp, crashing through prickly underbrush and pushing past low-hanging branches. The sun glinted off the Lion Prince's armor as he skidded to a halt.

"I know he's here, Cragger!" Laval cried out in a loud voice. "What have you done with him?"

Laval's words echoed out over the swamp. A moment later, several Croc heads rose above the surface of the dark water. They swam menacingly toward the Lion Prince. Cragger, the Crocodile King, led them.

"I don't know what you're talking about, Laval," Cragger said in a smooth voice as he came onto the shore. "I haven't done anything with anyone."

"You're a liar," Laval said. "I know it was you mud-lovers who kidnapped Longtooth. Where is he? If you've hurt him, I swear by Chima—"

"Kidnapped?" Cragger interrupted. A toothy grin spread across his face. "Laval, Crocodiles don't kidnap anyone. We do, however, welcome new allies."

Several Crocs chuckled as Cragger gestured behind him. Laval followed Cragger's gaze and his jaw dropped. There was Longtooth, walking toward them, safe and sound.

"Longtooth!" Laval called out in relief. "Are you okay? I was so . . ." But his voice trailed off. Something about Longtooth's manner didn't seem right. The way he was sauntering over seemed quite comfortable, almost smug. He didn't look at all like he was in need of rescuing.

"Longtooth?" Laval asked.

The old Lion Warrior smiled. "I'm fine, Laval. My new friends wouldn't hurt me."

"Your new . . . friends?" Laval repeated. "I don't understand. I saw your guard post. It was a wreck, like there was a struggle. We thought—"

"That I'd been kidnapped?" Longtooth shook his head. "No, I was just in a rush to pack up and head to the Croc Swamp." He smiled. "I'm on their side now, Laval."

"What?" Laval gasped. He couldn't believe his ears. Had his father's most trusted guard really abandoned his own tribe?

Cragger, for his part, was enjoying this show immensely. Having one Lion walk into his swamp under a flag of truce was highly unusual. Having two Lions wander into camp on the same day was incredibly entertaining.

"I guess no one needs rescuing after all, Laval," Cragger sneered. "Why don't you head back to your Lion Camp. We'll be seeing you soon enough."

A Croc named Crug laughed from beside Cragger. "Yeah, that's right, Lion. With our new CHI-magnet weapon, your tribe doesn't stand a—"

"*Shhh!*" Cragger hissed at Crug. But it was too late. Laval had heard him.

"A new weapon?" Laval looked at Longtooth. "What's he talking about?"

Longtooth smiled. "Let's just say, I choose my allies wisely," he replied. "I heard rumors in the forest that the Crocs were about to become more powerful than ever. And I'll tell you this much. The new weapon on Cragger's Command Ship is quite . . . convincing." Longtooth and Cragger exchanged a knowing grin. "But I don't want to give away all the surprises."

Laval's eyes were wide with shock. "Longtooth, I don't understand," he pleaded. "You've been one of my dad's best guards for years. From before I was even born. We've fought side by side *against* the Crocs. For Chima, to protect the CHI! How could you do this?"

"Oh, that reminds me," Longtooth said. He reached deep into his satchel and handed Cragger a rolled up piece of parchment. "King Cragger, I meant to give this to you. It's a map of the Lion Temple, its secret passages, its guard posts," Longtooth glanced at Laval and snickered, "and everything you need to know in order to steal its CHI."

With those words, Laval snapped. He growled and clenched his fists. "You're a traitor!" he cried at Longtooth. "I won't let you get away with this!" Laval charged, almost knocking over Cragger in his rush to get at the Lion Warrior.

Snarling and yowling, the two Lions grappled with one another and fell into the mud. They tumbled over again and again in the best Lion fight Cragger had seen in a long time. Crug and Crawley rushed up to pull them apart, but Cragger stopped them.

"Let them go. It's about time someone put Laval in his place, and our new friend Longtooth is just the Lion to do it."

Over and over, Laval and Longtooth rolled, tearing through branches, knocking over pots of swamp grass, and crashing through racks of armor. Crocodiles scattered to avoid the flashing claws as the Lion Prince and old warrior battled.

Hearing the commotion, Crooler walked over to where Cragger, Crug, and Crawley were standing. "Brother, what's going on?" she asked.

Cragger chuckled. "Laval just found out that Longtooth is on our side now," he said. "And he was especially angry when Longtooth gave me this." Cragger held out the rolled up plans of the Lion Temple.

"Let me see that," Crooler said, taking the parchment away from Cragger. She unrolled it and studied the diagram. A second later, her eyes went wide. "Have you read these notes?" she snapped.

Cragger, his eyes still riveted by the fight, replied, "I was about to when Laval attacked Longtooth."

"It's all a trick!" Crooled cried. "Look at this parchment! This note says, 'Here's the spot where the Crocs get stomped.' And this one says, 'If you can read this, a big thanks from Laval.'"

"What?" Cragger exploded, ripping the parchment from her claws. He snarled. "What does this mean?"

"It means you let two Lions into our camp and they're wrecking the place!" yelled Crooler. "And they're headed for—oh, no!"

Oh, yes—the battle between the two Lions had carried them to where Cragger's Command Ship was docked. Longtooth grabbed Laval and flung him onto the deck of the vessel, right near where the CHI magnet was mounted. Then he leapt after the Lion Prince.

They smashed into the magnet, snapping the base in half. A few more slams and the whole structure fell apart, collapsing into the swamp.

Laval grabbed Longtooth's hand and pulled him to his feet. "Had enough?" he asked.

"I could keep this up all day," Longtooth replied, a knowing smile crossing his face. "But that weapon is finished . . . and it looks like we might be too unless we get out of here, fast."

Led by Cragger, the Crocodiles were charging the Command Ship. Laval gave a laugh and waved. "We heard a rumor you had a new weapon, but we couldn't figure out what it was and how to get close enough to wreck it. So thanks for inviting Longtooth in, Cragger, old buddy!"

With that, the two Lions sprang from the ship and ran as fast as they could through the jungle to where they had stowed two Speedorz. Behind them, they could hear the echoes of very, very angry Crocodiles. It was only when they had zipped well out of reach and back to the edge of the Lion Camp that Laval and Longtooth finally stopped, laughing uncontrollably.

"Next time, you get to be the traitor," Longtooth said, out of breath.

Laval shook himself, sending clumps of dirt flying in every direction. "Next time, try not to be so convincing. For a second there, you almost had me going. And *I* knew it was all a trick."

Longtooth chuckled. "Hey, you don't get to be my age without learning a few acting skills along the way."

"They came in handy," Laval agreed. "Now we know what the Crocs were up to. Let's go tell the Eagles about the CHI magnet. They'll know how to build a counter weapon, in case the Crocs try this again." Then, Laval looked Longtooth up and down and scrunched up his nose. "Next time, let's also fight someplace less muddy. You smell of swamp."

"You smell worse," Longtooth said.

"You hit like a baby Croc."

"You would know. Didn't you lose a fight to one once?"

Together, the two friends raced each other back to camp.

THE BEST OF ENEMIES

'm in a whole lot of trouble this time, thought Eris. *I got myself into this—now how do I get myself out?*

It was late afternoon in Chima. Eris had just finished picking up her monthly supply of CHI and was on her way back to the Eagle Compound when she heard a voice calling for help in the forest. Quickly, she had dove deep into the woods to take a closer look. But in a split second, she was ambushed by Worriz and Cragger! They took her CHI and threw her into a cage built out of swamp branches. She was trapped!

Now her two captors were carrying her through the forest, using poles they had attached to the bottom of the cage. They were headed for the Croc Swamp. From what they said, they planned to hold her for ransom.

"How much CHI do you think bird-beak over here is worth?" Worriz said with a wicked grin.

Cragger chuckled. "It depends. We could ransom her back to the Eagles . . . or her Lion friends. I'm sure when Laval hears his *girlfriend* is our prisoner, he'll come running."

"Hey, I'm not his girlfriend!" Eris snapped.

That only made Cragger and Worriz laugh harder.

"Looks like we ruffled her feathers!" Worriz cackled.

Eris was fuming, but she knew being angry or afraid wouldn't help matters. She had to stay calm and figure out a way to escape. *And* get her CHI pouch back. She snuck a closer look at cage door. It was tied shut tightly with rope. Eris was sure she could undo it if she had enough time. But she needed a way to distract Cragger and Worriz for longer than just a few chuckles. She focused again on what they were saying.

"Yeah," Cragger continued. "My plan is going perfectly. Instead of having to steal the Lion's CHI, they're going to bring it straight to us!"

Worriz's expression suddenly changed. "*Your* plan?" he said. "Don't you mean *my* plan? I'm the one who came up with the idea of kidnapping the Eagle."

"Well, I didn't see your Wolves building this cage out of swamp branches, did I?" Cragger snapped.

That gave Eris an idea. She glanced down at the bottom of her cage. A few stones were caught between the branches. She quietly picked one up. It was heavy.

While Cragger and Worriz were arguing, she threw the pebble onto the path behind them.

Crack!

"What was that?" Cragger asked, whipping around.

"Nothing," said Worriz. "Probably just a nut falling."

The next time Cragger and Worriz weren't looking, Eris threw another stone. This time she aimed it for a big tree trunk on the side of the path. It made an even louder noise.

CRACK!

"I think someone is out there," Cragger said, narrowing his eyes.

"It's probably Laval," said Eris. "Maybe he doesn't like seeing his girlfriend captured."

"Go see who it is," Cragger ordered Worriz.

Worriz glared at Cragger, but he went.

As soon as the Wolf was gone, Eris murmured under her breath, "I'm surprised you let him talk to you that way."

"You be quiet," Cragger snapped.

"Suit yourself," Eris said, with a shrug. "But I wouldn't stand for it."

Cragger's head whipped around. "What are you talking about?"

"What, did you really not hear?" Eris laughed. "You must have too much swamp water in your ears. The way he called you out on the plan. Acting like it was his idea. Did you hear the tone in his voice? I mean, it was like, like . . ."

"Like what?" Cragger asked.

"Like he was in charge," Eris finished.

"That's enough out of you," Cragger snarled. But his expression had grown dark. Eris could tell he was thinking about what she had said.

"I wouldn't worry about it," she added. "After all,

everyone knows you're the leader, not Worriz. Don't they?"

Cragger didn't reply. A moment later, Worriz returned. "I didn't see anything out there, and . . . hey, what's the matter with you?"

Cragger had stalked up to the Wolf until they were nose to nose. "Of course *you* didn't see anything," he snapped. "Because it takes a Croc to get anything done around here. Now, *I* will go in there, and *I* will find Laval. You stay here and guard the Eagle."

With that, Cragger stomped off into the jungle.

Worriz watched him go, shaking his head. "There must be something in that swamp water he's always wallowing in."

"Nah," said Eris. "He just didn't expect you to come back, that's all."

"Huh?" said Worriz.

"Well, I don't think he wanted you to know," Eris replied, "but he was just saying, 'Laval could beat Worriz with both paws tied behind his back and a sack over his head.' He figured if you didn't come back in ten minutes, he would just head off to the Croc Swamp alone with me."

"He wouldn't do that," said Worriz. Then he thought about it for a moment. "Would he?"

"With you out of the way, maybe somebody else would become leader of the Wolf pack," Eris continued. "Somebody Cragger could push around."

"Somebody Cragger could . . ." Worriz repeated. A low growl came from his throat. Just then, Cragger returned from the woods. He still looked angry.

"I didn't see anything," said the Croc. "Your bumbling around in there probably gave him a chance to hide. Let's get moving before he and his friends ambush us."

"You always like to be in charge, don't you?" said Worriz.

"That's right. I *am* in charge," Cragger shot back. "And you'd better get used to it, if you know what's good for you."

"Since when?" Worriz snarled angrily. "The Crocs wouldn't be anywhere if it weren't for the Wolves. We're the ones winning this battle for you. And we don't take orders from anyone!"

As the pair argued, Eris threw her last two rocks into the woods.

CRACK! CRACK!

The noises echoed so loudly that Cragger and Worriz jumped and dropped her cage onto the ground.

"Okay, now somebody *is* in there," said Worriz.

"I thought you Wolves could smell a Lion from a mile away," Cragger taunted him.

"I could, if the stink of swamp water on you wasn't so strong," Worriz shot back.

"Go see who's following us," demanded Cragger.

"Oh, you'd like that, wouldn't you?" Worriz said. "Why don't you go?"

"Fine," said Cragger. "We'll *both* go. This Eagle isn't escaping anytime soon. You go first."

Worriz, who had started walking toward the woods, stopped dead. "I'm not turning my back on you again. You go first."

"Why not go side by side?" Eris said with a shrug from her cage.

The Wolf and the Croc glared at one another and tried that, only to find themselves wedged between two big trees. With a great deal of grunting, they managed to continue on into the woods.

The moment they were out of eyesight, Eris worked fast. She undid the rope, and then she wrapped it loosely around again so it would look like it was still tied. She could have just flown off, but she needed her CHI back. And she knew just how to get it.

Worriz and Cragger were still arguing when they returned. Again, they hadn't spotted any Lions. They were frustrated and angry.

"Oh, you're alone?" Eris said, sounding surprised. "Didn't they find you?"

"Who?" said Cragger. "What are you talking about?"

"Crawley and Crug," Eris answered. "They were carrying that big sack and lots of rope like you wanted . . . oops, I probably shouldn't say anymore. Anyway, they're looking for you in the woods. Wilhurt and Windra are, too. They showed up just after."

Cragger and Worriz turned to glare at each other. By now, they had forgotten about their victory in capturing Eris. Both were focused on the other and what sneaky thing he might be planning.

"What are you up to, Swamp Breath?" Worriz growled.

"Me? How about you?" Cragger demanded.

"Scale-head!"

"Furball!"

They were so intent on their argument that neither one noticed Eris slip out of her cage. In one quick motion, she snatched the CHI pouch from behind Cragger and flew off into the air. "So long, guys!" she cried out happily.

"Hey!" said Cragger. "She's getting away!"

"Oh, great," said Worriz. "You were so busy planning how to get rid of me that you completely forgot about watching our real prisoner."

"I never said I wanted to get rid of you!" Cragger exploded. "You're the one who's trying take charge over me!"

"Don't play stupid," Worriz said. "I know all about your plan."

"What plan?!" Cragger roared. "The only plan was to ransom that Eagle for CHI. And now she's escaped!"

Worriz snarled. "Sure, and if I happened to have an 'accident' or 'get captured' by the Lions along the way, all the better for you. That Eagle told me—"

"You must have fur in your brain! You couldn't stand taking orders from me. That Eagle said—"

Suddenly, both Cragger and Worriz stopped and looked at one another. They grew very quiet. Then, slowly, they began to growl. It became louder and louder until they were both roaring:

"ERIIIIIS!"

Their cry echoed out over the forest. Eris, by this point well out of danger, heard it faintly and smiled to herself. *Looks like they figured it out*, she thought. *Guess the joke's on them. Hope they have a sense of humor. Because with friends like that, who needs enemies?*

THE VAULT

"**L**ongtooth! Wake up!"

The old Lion Warrior sat up abruptly. "I wasn't napping," Longtooth insisted, half asleep. "I was just . . . resting my eyes."

Leonidas was standing over him. He shook Longtooth fully awake. "I needed to find you!" Leonidas exclaimed. "Because . . . um . . . because . . ."

Longtooth sighed. Leonidas was never very good at doing two things at once, like bringing a message and remembering what it was.

"Are we under attack?" Longtooth asked groggily.

"No," said Leonidas. "That's not it."

"Is the CHI in danger?"

"No, not that," Leonidas replied. He furrowed his brow in concentration.

"Think!" said Longtooth, exasperated. "Did Laval send you to find me?"

"That's it!" cried Leonidas. "Laval! CHI! Laval is trapped in the legendary CHI vault!"

Longtooth slowly rose to his feet. He already missed the nap he wasn't going to get to finish. "All right," he said, yawning. "You had better start from the beginning."

As Longtooth gathered his CHI harness and armor, Leonidas explained what had happened. A few weeks before, while Laval had been cleaning out the map room as part of his chores, he had stumbled across a particularly old-looking scroll. It belonged to the Lion Elders. The scroll told of an ancient legend about a CHI vault the Lions had built centuries ago, the last time the CHI was in danger.

According to the legend, the vault was filled with doom traps and was one of the most secure places ever created to store CHI. But when the danger passed, the Lions never needed to use their treacherous vault after all.

So it remained hidden somewhere in the forest. Laval asked the Elders about the legend, and they said it was just a myth. But Laval insisted that if it was real, it could be the perfect solution for protecting the CHI.

"Laval used the scroll and the Lion Elders' maps to figure out where the CHI vault might be," Leonidas explained. "I saw him sneaking out of the Compound this morning. Laval made me promise not to say anything. But he hasn't been back all day. I'm worried something might have happened to him."

"All right," said Longtooth as they prepared to set out. "Where's this legendary CHI vault so we can go and find him?"

Leonidas's expression suddenly went blank. "*Uhhhh*, find him. Right . . ." he said.

Longtooth sighed. "You mean you don't know where he went? How are we going to rescue him if we don't know where he is?"

Leonidas scratched his head with a rolled up parchment he held in one hand. "I'm not sure," he said slowly. "I feel like Laval told me before he left, but now I can't remember."

Longtooth gently took the parchment from Leonidas's paw and unrolled it. It was one of the Lion Elders' maps, with a trail drawn on it.

"Did Laval by any chance give you this?" Longtooth asked.

Leonidas brightened. "Oh, yeah! He did. Good thinking, Longtooth. I completely forgot!"

Torches in hand, Leonidas and Longtooth reached the entrance to the ancient CHI vault marked on the map. At least, it was where the entrance was supposed to be.

Longtooth glanced down at the map and back up to the weathered, root-ridden rock crevice in front of them. He frowned. "Is this really it? It just looks like an old hole in the rocks."

Leonidas shrugged. "I guess there's only one way to find out."

The two Lions advanced inside. Except for the glow of their torches, there was no light to guide their way. They had gone only a short distance when Leonidas's eyes suddenly grew wide. "Hey!" he said. "Look at that. I didn't know you could grow grass in a cave with no light."

"Grass in a—?" Longtooth started.

Before Longtooth could stop him, Leonidas headed for the grassy spot in the middle of the narrow tunnel. As soon as he put one paw on the grass, it caved in, revealing a deep pit below. Leonidas started to tumble in! Longtooth lunged forward and grabbed his friend before he could fall.

"Doom traps, remember?" said Longtooth. "I'm pretty sure the key word there is *doom*. We have to be more careful."

"That was a close one," Leonidas breathed. "Thanks." Then, his face grew worried. "I sure hope Laval is okay."

"Me, too," said Longtooth. "Let's keep going."

Backing up a few steps, the two Lions took a running jump and just made it over the pit. They kept walking, until they came to a much wider part of the cave. On the left-hand side of the stone floor there was a vine tied into a loop. The vine trailed up toward the ceiling.

"Okay, now that one's too obvious," said Longtooth. "Why would you step into that vine? Of course it will hoist you up toward the ceiling. All we have to do is go around it."

Longtooth took a few steps to the right of the vine. Just as he was beside the loop, the stone floor under his feet sank a few inches. A big slab of rock suddenly shot out from the cave wall, big enough to crush him against the opposite side.

"This way!" yelled Leonidas. He grabbed Longtooth and pulled him into the center of the vine loop. The vine yanked up, pulled tight around their legs, and jerked them into the air just as the slab crashed against the wall.

"You're right," said Leonidas. "It was way too obvious. Anybody could see you were supposed to step into it to get pulled up to the ceiling. Right?"

"Um, right," said Longtooth. "I was just showing you why you would want to be up near the ceiling."

The vine slowly lowered the two back down to the floor. Longtooth and Leonidas freed themselves and started forward again.

As they walked, Longtooth grumbled to himself. He was worried about Laval. He was also annoyed with the Lion Prince for getting into this mess. But as much as Longtooth's aches and pains were bothering him, he was beginning to look forward to the next trap. He was starting to see this whole thing as a big tactical challenge. And if there was one thing Longtooth was always up for, it was a challenge.

They had walked a little ways farther when Leonidas spotted something. "There's a pile of CHI against that wall. Maybe Laval dropped it? Or maybe it's another trap?"

Longtooth thought hard. It did look like an obvious trap, but the last time, the obvious trap turned out not to be one at all. So maybe this one was safe . . . or maybe the ancient builders of the vault just wanted him to think it was safe . . . but they would know he would never believe it wasn't a trap, so maybe it *was* safe. This was starting to make Longtooth's head hurt.

He knelt down to examine the CHI. Suddenly, one of the orbs flew out at him. He moved aside and it smacked against the cave wall with a loud thud.

"That's not CHI!" exclaimed Longtooth. "It's a rock painted to look like CHI."

"Wow, there are CHI rocks now?" exclaimed Leonidas. "Awesome!"

More of the rocks flew out at the two Lions from a miniature catapult hidden beneath the pile.

"Leonidas! Run!" yelled Longtooth. They sprinted down the tunnel to avoid the barrage.

Up ahead, a sticky net was drooping low from the ceiling. Both Lions hit the floor and rolled underneath it. It was a good thing they were down low, too, because just past the nets, stone spikes started flying out of the walls above their heads.

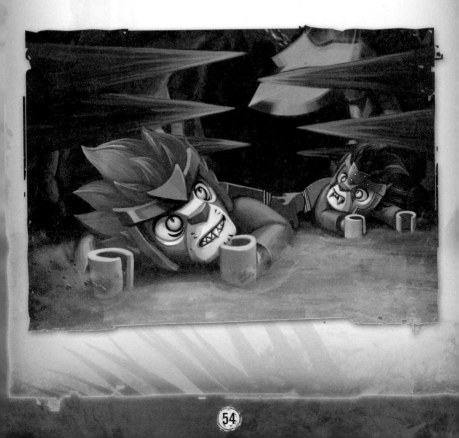

"How did the Lions who invented this vault ever make it through to get to the CHI they stored?" grumbled Longtooth.

The friends crawled forward until they were past the spikes. Longtooth sat with his back to the cave wall, breathing heavily. He was exahusted. Leonidas, on the other hand, still seemed full of energy.

"Not sure how much farther we have to go," said Longtooth. "There might be a dozen traps between here and the vault door. We might be sitting in thc middle of one right now. So why don't you look more worried?"

Leonidas shrugged. "I just take things one at a time," he said. "I sometimes try to take things two at a time, but that gets confusing. And you remember what happened when I took things *four* at a time."

Longtooth winced. He did remember. It took a week to clean up that mess, and everyone's fur smelled of swamp for a month.

Together, the two Lions started walking again. They came to a massive wooden door with a big keypad in its center and a handle on the right. This had to be the door to the vault itself.

Longtooth immediately began trying different combinations, but none of them worked. After each

combination, he would push the door handle down and try to pull it open, but the door wouldn't budge. He started to feel very frustrated. Minutes went by, then an hour as he tried and tried to solve this last puzzle. When Leonidas suggested he take a break, Longtooth angrily answered that he would beat this challenge yet.

Leonidas waited until Longtooth stopped for a moment. Then he reached out, and tried pulling the handle *upward*. The door opened.

"Things that look like traps aren't," said Leonidas. "Things that look safe aren't. So I figured maybe something that looked like it was a normal, locked door . . . wasn't."

"And the vault builders guessed an intruder would be so angry by the time he got here, he would spend hours trying to find a combination that didn't exist," realized Longtooth.

Now they were faced with another door. It looked almost identical to the previous one. The only difference was the last keypad had numbers and this one had letters. Just as a precaution, Longtooth tried the handle up and down, but this door remained locked tight.

"Can I try?" asked Leonidas.

"Sure," said Longtooth.

Leonidas started using the keypad to spell out every word he could think of that might be the combination: *Lion*, *CHI*, *Chima*, *Legend Beast*, even *Vault*. None of them were right.

"Boy, they sure made this hard," he said finally. "The ancient Lions must have really wanted to keep their enemies out."

Longtooth smiled. "Leonidas . . . nothing is what you expect in here. Think about it: If you wanted a combination no enemy would ever guess, what would you use?"

Leonidas thought for a moment. Then he punched the letters on the keypad to spell:

W-E-L-C-O-M-E

The door swung open. There was Laval, standing in the middle of the vault. He smiled broadly at the sight of his two friends.

"Am I glad to see you!" he exclaimed happily.

"Laval!" Leonidas cried.

"Are you okay?" asked Longtooth.

"I am now." Laval breathed a sigh of relief. "I wasn't sure anyone would ever reach me. I guess I shouldn't have tried to find this vault on my own."

"Might have been a good idea," Longtooth said.

"How did you make it past all those doom traps?" Leonidas asked, amazed. "They almost got us . . . several times! I wouldn't have made it through if Longtooth wasn't with me."

Longtooth nodded. "Leonidas saved my hide a few times, too. How did you get past them?"

Laval chuckled and pointed up at the ceiling. "I didn't have to. I fell in from up there."

Longtooth and Leonidas followed his gaze upward. High up on the vault ceiling was a cluster of tightly packed rocks that looked like they were blocking a large opening.

"There was a hole up there from the outside when I got here," Laval explained. "The rocks have probably been wearing away for hundreds of years. When I lowered myself in, they collapsed and the hole was blocked. The vault door was sealed from the outside, so I would have been trapped in here forever." He smiled gratefully at his two friends. "If it wasn't for you two."

"Wow," Leonidas said. "I can't believe you missed all those doom traps. They were really something!"

Laval put his arms around each of their shoulders. "Well, I guess I'll get to see them on the way out of this vault." He smiled. "But as long as I have you two by my side, I'm pretty sure we can handle anything."